# THE FLAT

*Spiritual Fiction*

## NANIMA SERIES
### BOOK IV

## DONNA GODDARD

# CONTENTS

# PART II
# TIME IS UP

# PART I
# SIX MONTHS AT A TIME

# PAPERBOY

# CHAPTER 1

## HAPPY DREAMS

"Happy dreams," said Luna as he opened the bedroom door for Iggy to enter.

"Sleep well," said Maliyan as she headed for the bathroom.

"I will," said Luna. "The night is so quiet at your house that I feel like I'm in a cocoon."

He was used to the hustle and bustle, traffic and horns, yelling and late-night laughing of inner-city life.

At the end of his Christmas holiday break, Luna was ready to tell Maliyan that he wasn't in the northern city, but still in the southern one near her. When he initially decided to move back north, he gave notice on his flat. By the time he decided that he was no longer going, his flat had been leased to someone else, so he was homeless. Maliyan offered him her spare room, assuming he wouldn't take it. He did take it. The last time they lived together was summer, two years ago, in Nanima, in the shophouse of Luna Tiks.

# CHAPTER 2

# STILL ALIVE

In his first week of living in The Flat, Luna visited every cafe in town. He was unimpressed by all, some more than others. The Flat didn't have a happening cafe like Sonder in Black Forest. Its cafes were conventional country ones, at best, clean, pleasant, and running smoothly. None had a vibe—not the vibe that suited Luna.

The worst one was *Paperboy*. It had become old and worn long ago, as had its owner, who was an original paperboy from the area when there was no freeway. The disgruntled man, in his mid-seventies, took a shine to Luna. He was won over when Luna decided to have his coffee at one of the tables and listened to some of his worn-out stories. Luna knew which jokes the man would like—rough and ready, crass and offensive—and that clinched it.

As he left, Luna said, "I've been a cafe owner myself. It's a hard slog."

The paperboy mumbled to himself and then looked hard at his new mate.

"Well, matey, if ever you feel like getting back into it,

let me know," said the paperboy. "Before I die, I want to visit Italy. It's been a lifelong dream, but if I don't do it soon, my time will be done."

Luna looked around the cafe with its peeling wallpaper and empty seats. He noticed that the coffee machine was new. The paperboy's eyes, sharper than what he gave away, tracked Luna's gaze and faint interest.

His energy picked up, and he said, "The old one broke. I had to get a new one. Look, buddy, if you are interested, you could have the place for six months for next to nothing and make of it what you can. Then I could go to Italy, and it would still be alive when I return, that is, if *I'm* still alive."

## CHAPTER 3

### INCLUSIVENESS

After thinking about the paperboy's offer for a few days and discussing it with Maliyan, Luna decided to accept it and became the new, if temporary, owner of Paperboy. He quickly acquired the keys and set about cleaning it. After throwing out a mass of dirty stuff lying around the premises, he stuffed the rest in the back shed. He then bought ten cheap, bright cushions and some potted plants on sale and placed them strategically around the room. He visited the Country Women's Association Op Shop next to Maliyan and found some quaint cups, saucers, plates, and ornaments. By the end of the week, Paperboy was a relatively transformed place.

Now, for the tricky bit—staff. You don't need staff when you don't have customers, but Luna intended to have both. He talked one of his chef friends into coming out to The Flat to cook for six months. Then, he set his mind on winning over the town's young people who would become his rotating hospitality staff. Like moths to a flame, they gravitated to Luna's funny and engaging ways. Even in his mid-forties, he still possessed a coolness that young people are drawn to.

He quickly monopolised the gay community's work-base. A lot of diverse people came to The Flat, and amongst them was a fairly significant gay population. Being so close to the city, people came who wanted to escape city life but also have access to it. These days, small businesses must be diligent about fulfilling all the increasingly mandated inclusive policies, but Luna was the personification of inclusiveness. Inclusiveness means including someone, as they are, into ourselves. His inclusiveness was what made his relationship with Maliyan possible.

# CHAPTER 4

## SHAKANA

"I know what the dream planet is called," said Bell on the phone. "I went there in my dream last night, and a Wise One told me. They said it translates as Shakana."

"Really?" said Maliyan.

"The Wise One said that they don't have names for each other or even for their planet because everything is known as energy," said Bell. "However, the word Shakana is close because it means empathic collective consciousness, which is what they are."

*In Bell's dream of planet Shakana:*

"Breathe in and out three times, slowly," said the Wise One. "As you breathe out, see your mind, consciousness, and soul expanding. Let it grow more each time. Think of yourself as a translucent, giant, blue ball of harmonic, shining energy. Watch as your spread and size increase. You are full of light.

A tiny shape is in the centre of the massive ball of light. It is the shape of a human body. It is your body. It is your body in crystallised form. Contrary to your normal perceptual belief, your mind is not inside your body. It is the other way around. It is your body that is in your mind.

The crystal substance that forms your body can be reformed in a different way. Whenever you expand your consciousness and move your energy beyond your body's boundaries, the material of your physical body can restructure itself more healthily.

Imagine yourself in perfect health. You know what that feels like, don't you? It can be like not feeling anything. Nothing is grating or clunking. Everything is operating smoothly, like an oiled machine. The body becomes silent. Strong and silent. Have a clear image of your body in perfect health, and then, with your consciousness enlarged, imprint that on the crystalline substance that forms your body.

For this exercise to work effectively, repeat it often during your day-to-day Earth life, not because it can't be instantaneous, but because you believe it can't be. The problem is not the process but your ingrained and unconscious belief patterns. Your old belief systems will keep reversing the body back into its preferred, comfortable, dysfunctional version. If you persevere and keep replanting the new ideas, your body will slowly but surely reform and restructure itself, and sometimes, it will make big, sudden leaps."

"THE WISE ONE TOLD ME THAT OUR BODY IS IN OUR mind, not the other way around," said Bell. "How strange to think of it like that."

"Yes," said Maliyan, "and it's not only our body that is in our mind. There is more in our mind than there is *out there*."

CHAPTER 5

# QUEERER THAN QUEER

"By the way," said Maliyan as Bell was about to hang up the phone, "Luna is living with me."

"Living with you?" said Bell. "Why?"

"He's working in The Flat for six months."

"Is he staying with you for six months?"

"I'm not sure how long he is staying."

After a pause, Bell said, "I don't think that will work."

"It is working," said Maliyan.

"In what way is it working?"

"In whatever way it decides to work."

"He's gay," said Bell.

"Well then, he won't bother me for sex."

"Is that a good thing?"

"Maybe, maybe not," said Maliyan.

"You might not need it, but he probably does. What if he starts bringing male company home?"

"He won't."

BEFORE LUNA BEGAN STAYING AT MALIYAN'S HOUSE, SHE told him, "I am a highly perceptive and intuitive person, Luna, and I have set up my life so that other people's energy doesn't adversely affect me. My home is my energetic sanctuary. You can be here, but not your friends. Sorry, you need to meet up with them somewhere else."

Although Maliyan understood other people's need to socialise, she had none. That's what happens when you are entirely self-assured on the inside. Your interactions with people become very purposeful and decisive. It's not disengagement. You are totally connected, but it is conscious connection.

"LUNA IS ONLY QUEER IN ONE WAY," MALIYAN SAID TO Bell. "I'm queer in just about every way except that one."

# HEALER

## CHAPTER 6

## FEELER

When Maliyan moved to The Flat, she decided to use one of her three bedrooms as a workspace. She hadn't worked for the past three years, since moving to the country. In Nanima, she bought a small home and lived off her savings. She neither needed nor wanted much in the way of material things, so, at a scrape, it was viable, at least, for some years. When she moved to Black Forest, she rented Bell's father's house. Eventually, her Nanima house was sold, and the money was invested. Now that she was in The Flat, she was still renting and had a basic income from her investments. Nevertheless, she decided to go back to work.

Maliyan didn't return to her clerical work of thirty years in the city. She was drawn to something new—healing. It wasn't the money. She wasn't even sure if she would make any money. It was the desire to help, and she found the idea exciting. The field of healing is so obscure that anyone can say they are a healer. The goods speak for themselves. She made an online site and trusted that the right people would find her. They did.

Her healing room had two chairs for clients, a massage table for hands-on healing (or Reiki), a desk, and an area that acted as a sacred space. It had candles, burning oil, incense, chimes, bells, and a few favourite spiritual books and images. In the corner was a rolled-up yoga mat and cushion for yoga asanas, meditations, prayer, and any other spiritual practice that took Maliyan's fancy.

With time, the atmosphere in the room became highly charged from daily spiritual practices, which was exactly what she wanted it to be for prospective clients. Not that Maliyan had guests, but the room would have been too charged for visitors to sleep in. They would have had too many vivid dreams, and many would not have been pleasant. A healing space not only heals but also brings things up to be healed. Luna was somewhat suspicious of the room and never went in it, even when Maliyan sat there. He would stand at the door and talk to her.

Maliyan's clients usually came during the day when Luna was at Paperboy, but occasionally, he was home. Once, Maliyan told him to stay in his room for one hour and be quiet so the client wouldn't know anyone was home. People tend to be very secretive about their problems, although energetically, there is no such thing as privacy.

The next time a client came in the evening, Maliyan said to Luna, "You'll have to go for a walk for an hour."

"I'll stay in my room again," said Luna.

"No, that doesn't work."

"Why? They can't hear me."

"It's energy," said Maliyan. "I need the energy in the whole house to be a certain way."

Insulted, Luna huffed off and banged the door. Not a great start to a healing session.

When the session ended and Luna returned home, Maliyan said, "It's your home too, for as long as you want it to be. I won't book anyone in at night."

Luna nodded and went to his room, and that was that.

# CHAPTER 7

# BARRY

## SWEEP YOU OFF YOUR FEET

Maliyan's first client was Barry, a seventy-year-old deaf man. That was a challenge. How do you communicate concepts to a person who can't hear words?

As it turned out, he was an excellent lipreader from fifty years of practice. He had hearing until he was twenty and then lost nearly all of it with an infection. He was talkative and avoided watching your face if he didn't want to stop talking.

*How convenient!* thought Maliyan. *If he was in an argument [which he often was with his long-term wife], he could refuse to look at the other person's lips and thus not "hear" them.*

Malayan surmised that he probably only came to her because she offered a large price reduction to pensioners. Nevertheless, it didn't take him long to realise that Maliyan may be useful to him.

"I might be deaf," said Barry, "but I'm not dumb."

"Of course not," said Maliyan.

His life was a mess of drama, blame, anger, and sadness. He had disjointed relationships with all four grown daughters. His wife left him seven years ago. However, he had the demeanour of someone whose spouse had recently abandoned the relationship.

At one point, he mentioned that he was a good ballroom dancer in his late teens.

"Can you hear the beat of music if it's loud?" asked Maliyan.

"Yes, I can hear it a bit with my hearing aid," said Barry.

"What was your favourite music when you danced?" asked Maliyan.

"The Platters!" said Barry.

After quickly searching her music app, Maliyan started playing *Heaven on Earth* by The Platters and turned it to full volume. She jumped up and stretched out her hand to him.

"Come," she said, "let's dance."

There was no problem with him paying attention to her lips now. Surprised and nervous, he nevertheless took her hand and got up. Not sure how much he could hear the beat and how much he could remember the steps, Maliyan assumed she would have to take the lead. However, after a few minutes, Barry's tall, stiff body relaxed and took the lead perfectly in time with the music. They slowly moved around the room for five more minutes.

Then, Maliyan released her hold and told Barry that they would do some healing. He needed to lie down and close his eyes for the healing. As he couldn't see, he also couldn't "hear", so everything had to be transferred energetically, without language cues. When the hands-on healing was finished, Barry wanted to talk more, much more, but Maliyan stopped him.

"See how you go over the next few weeks," said Maliyan, "and we'll talk again if you wish to return."

She didn't need to worry about him wanting to come back. He started messaging her every day. He explained that because he was on a pension, he could only afford to come once a fortnight, and couldn't even really afford that. He asked if he could come and pay later. He asked if he could "drop in" and talk. He went into long explanations about why no one understands him.

TEXT FROM BARRY

I'm sorry for bothering you so much. If you give me a chance, I could sweep you off your feet.

He was entirely inappropriate but harmless. Anyway, Maliyan felt that those who came to her were meant to come. It was not for her to say who would come, what the starting point was, or what steps the person would take for their own healing. Her replies consisted of silence or brief, professional replies.

MALIYAN

No, you cannot call in. When you can afford it again, please book a session.

He managed to come a few more times. A senior pension does not allow for "luxuries" such as private professional sessions of anything, even with big discounts. But if people are given things too easily, they will often take advantage of them. The thing will tend to lose its worth, and the recipient will not get what they could have out of it. So, it's a balance.

In his last session, Barry brought a letter he had written to his ex-wife, which had not yet been sent. It was smothered in self-pity. By this stage, Maliyan was able to explain to him that he needed to focus on his wife's needs and feelings if he wanted to restore any sort of relationship with her. Together, they completely reworded the letter.

"Women are good at this sort of thing," said Barry. "Men aren't."

That was the last time Maliyan saw Barry. Maybe things improved with his ex-wife, and he no longer needed help in the same way. Maybe he didn't want to spend his valuable pension on his own growth. Either way, no one ever returns to their previous state of consciousness. It's a process of forwards and backwards. The backwards consolidates growth and allows it to settle into our being. The forwards is for freedom.

# CHAPTER 8

# CARMEL

## LIKE IT LIKE THAT

Another client was a neighbour of Maliyan's who was in her late eighties. She was small in stature and round in diameter, as many older people become. They move less, but their food intake doesn't decrease enough to match their lack of movement. They shrink in height and grow in width. A friendly, grandmotherly sort of woman, Carmel one day asked Maliyan what work she did and then decided to book in.

She walked slowly from next door to her appointment using her walking frame. Although she struggled to walk, she was frequently out and about in her little red car, zooming here and there between her eight children and many grandchildren. She said she couldn't sit still.

"Do you still have your husband with you?" asked Maliyan in the session.

"Not for the last two years," said Carmel.

"I'm sorry to hear that," said Maliyan.

"Don't be," said Carmel. "After sixty-eight years, I left the old fool. I couldn't stand it anymore."

*Sixty-eight years is a long time after which to decide that you cannot stand someone anymore,* thought Maliyan.

"He's not that bad, I s'pose", said Carmel, "but I wanted my freedom. So, I moved out of our house and rent here."

Carmel was not the sort of person to say mean things about people in general. Maliyan guessed that it was only her husband that she allowed herself to speak about in such a way. She often saw Carmel's children and grandchildren pulling up to or leaving her house. Just yesterday, she heard one of the adult grandchildren yell out their car window, "Love you, Nan!"

"How is it all working then?" asked Maliyan.

"Fine. I still see my hubby a lot. Sometimes, I stay there, and sometimes he stays here. But I can always leave or tell him to leave. And I like it like that."

"Well, why not?" said Maliyan.

"The family home has just been sold," said Carmel. "Half the money is not enough for me to buy around here, so I'll keep renting. But damn fool hubby has bought somewhere way out country, three hours away. Cheaper out there, you see. But who's going to drive three hours to visit him? I guess it'll be me."

"How can I help you today?" asked Maliyan.

Carmel had a long list of physical problems. She wasn't very receptive to new ideas (physical or spiritual), although she had been receptive to the unusual idea of leaving her relatively compatible husband after sixty-eight years. Maliyan did a short healing with Carmel sitting in the chair. She put on soft, conventional music (no chanting, drums, chimes, or ethereal chords) and helped her relax with deep breathing. That was about the best she could hope for at this stage.

Knowing that her body was the most accessible point of helping her, Maliyan said, "Have you ever been to a chiropractor?"

"No," said Carmel. "I'm not into stuff like that. Anyway, I'm going to see the surgeon next week."

"I see," said Maliyan.

Carmel considered the state of her body as an inevitable part of ageing. Maliyan knew it was not. It is possible and highly desirable for people to look after their bodies well enough over a lifetime to avoid many, if not most, illnesses. Old age doesn't have to be frailty, pain, suffering, and a brutal collapse of material existence. It can be gentle, vital, wise, peaceful, and active. The soul can exit the body calmly and efficiently at the right time without undue stress. Carmel was a long way from that, but nevertheless, could be helped with a few simple changes.

"I think you would be surprised how much a chiropractor could help you," said Maliyan. "It wouldn't be an instant fix, but if you went every week, the pain in your body would significantly reduce. I can see how crooked your hips are, and that is causing your sciatica."

Maliyan didn't overload her with more information about how it would help her organs and nervous system, and allow for a better flow of energy along the spine so that her life force would not have to fight itself. Carmel looked unconvinced, but that was her right to be. Healing has to be allowed into one's life, not forced.

# CHAPTER 9

# CLARA

## FROM EARTH AND HEAVEN

Clara was a healer herself. She booked an online session as she could not travel to Maliyan. She cared for her elderly parents in her hometown, which she hated. She hated the town, not her parents, although she increasingly resented having to look after them. Clara was usually very active with many ideas and lots of energy. Six months ago, after accepting an interesting job overseas, she went to say goodbye to her parents. However, she realised she couldn't leave them alone after seeing them. She now felt utterly stuck and resentful (unusual feelings for her).

Maliyan was not sure how receptive Clara was to her help because people in the same profession can sometimes be a little snooty and judgmental of each other. Not that Clara was like that, but her demeanour was slightly guarded. Nevertheless, they talked about the ideas of freedom and honesty and the possible practical ways to resolve the problem. As the session was online, there was no hands-on healing. The healing aspect had to be an entirely nonphysical transfer of energy, negating space and time. At the end of the session, Clara was politely grateful and ended the conversation.

Two weeks later, Maliyan heard from a different Clara altogether. She said it was like a miracle. The entire weight of the situation had lifted, and she felt reconnected to her true self. She got an idea about how to lessen her care duties with her parents and gradually get them used to outside help. Out of the blue, she was offered another wonderful job overseas. It was better than the one she had to decline, allowing her to further her spiritual development. Furthermore, they were willing to wait for her.

Lastly, she said that the strangest thing happened to her bank account. Lack of money was one of her pressing problems due to her inability to work. She didn't even have enough to pay Maliyan the full amount and asked for a discount, to which, of course, Maliyan said yes. From seemingly nowhere, a considerable amount of money landed in her account. She couldn't understand where on earth it had come from. The mysterious money sat in her account for a while, and as no one claimed it, she accepted it as a gift from Heaven. She immediately paid Maliyan the rest of the money, amongst other things.

"I was absolutely overwhelmed when I rang you," said Clara. "I woke up the next day as a new, calm, clear person. The constant anxiety that had been hounding me vanished. I don't know how to thank you."

"That's thanks enough," said Maliyan.

No healer heals anyone. No healer makes miracles. No healer is responsible for anyone's lack of receptivity or unwillingness to change. All a healer can do is get themselves in a healed state, and then it is up to the other person to be inspired to match that vibration or to prefer their misery. It's that simple. That beautiful. That powerful. Miracles are natural when we see life as energy. It is suffering that is so unnatural.

# WATERMELON SPECIAL

# CHAPTER 10

# THE SCONE MAN AND THE PANCAKE LADY

Once a month, The Flat had a town market. Vendors came from near and far. Their diverse range of goods, many handmade with love and natural ingredients, drew a crowd of customers from equally near and far. Maliyan watched as the scone man prepared a large batch of sultana scones for the oven. As she couldn't decide between the scone man and the pancake lady, she bought both, along with some liquorice from the liquorice man and some fudge from the fudge family.

After making her way through the maze of stalls, she weaved through the crowds on the adjoining street. Most of the cafes were busy with the overflow of market customers. She could see Luna through the front window of Paperboy, eyes on the many concurrent tasks of keeping a busy cafe running. People who work in hospitality keep relatively fit from running around all day. They also keep a fit mind as they have to think fast and remember a succession of orders and tasks—fast feet, fast mind—a good discipline.

Although Luna always complained about working in hospitality, it helped him stay on track. He was forced to be positive and engaged, whether he felt like it or not. Left to his own devices, it would have been a great deal more of *not feeling like it*. The survival of his business made him discipline his mind and emotions. In return, hundreds of people felt better for visiting his cafe. He couldn't see that, but one day, he would. Then, he probably wouldn't even have to work in hospitality if he didn't want to. It would have served its purpose. Seeing Maliyan out of the corner of his eye, he sighed. Last night was a restless one.

CHAPTER 11

# WATERMELON TOURMALINE

*ast night:*

It was 4:00 a.m., and Maliyan heard bumping in the kitchen.

"What are you doing?" she asked as she struggled to get her arms into her inside-out dressing gown sleeves.

"I can't sleep," said Luna. "I've been awake for the last hour."

It is no coincidence that many restless sleepers and troubled minds wake between 3:00 and 4:00 a.m. It is a time of high psychic sensitivity. That means that the mind will be working overtime with worries, unresolved issues, and fear. On the other hand, it is also a heightened time of out-of-body travels, lucid dreaming, inspired problem-solving, and brilliant ideas. Some of our most innovative scientific discoveries have come from 3:00 a.m. dreams and visions.

If you are the former, not the latter (the restless, not the inspired), you most likely won't want to wake up. You will be trying to get back to sleep, which won't work.

"Is anything bothering you?" asked Maliyan coaxingly.

"Nothing," said Luna. "Nothing at all."

"Okay. Well, what have you been thinking about for the last hour? You must have been thinking about something."

"If you must know—watermelon juice special."

"Hmm?"

"We have a watermelon juice special at Paperboy, and I can't get it out of my head."

Maliyan put the kettle on for herbal tea and said quietly, "You know, love, when a thought won't stop circling in our head, it really has nothing to do with the thing that is circling."

Luna looked doubtful but also desperate.

"How do I get rid of it?" he asked.

"Don't try to get rid of it. Listen to it."

Luna's attention was fading. Maliyan touched his arm, and he raised his head.

"I just want it to stop," he said. "I have to work tomorrow."

"I understand," said Maliyan, "but the watermelon is covering for something."

"Covering something? What sort of something?"

She could easily have told him what was "wrong" and what it was covering, but what good would that have been? Evolution has to happen by personal experience, not by someone telling us. Otherwise, it is powerless.

"I'm not sure," said Maliyan. "But you will know. Let it come up when it is ready. The watermelon is trying to help you."

"I'll try," said Luna with a sigh as he walked back to his room, herbal tea in hand. "I guess it will show its true colours when it's ready."

THE NEXT MORNING, MALIYAN PASSED LUNA A SMALL crystal before he went to work.

"What is it?" asked Luna.

"Watermelon tourmaline," answered Maliyan.

Luna held it to the light and said, "It's pink in the middle and green on the outside, like watermelon."

"Yes, the two colours of the heart—pink and green," said Maliyan. "It connects with the emotional centre."

After picking up the box that the crystal came in, Luna read:

*Watermelon tourmaline will help you connect with your feelings. It will soften the emotional space around you and bring closeness to your relationships.*

He put it in his pocket and kissed her goodbye.

# CHAPTER 12

# POPPING THE SEED

Although he momentarily considered it, Luna didn't deep dive into an emotional-heart transition. Instead, he left the watermelon tourmaline on the kitchen bench and got mean. That's one of the things that can happen when someone's higher self tries to talk to them but gets ignored.

It's like squeezing a watermelon seed. How much pressure does a watermelon seed need to pop? How much pressure can a person tolerate before releasing themselves to change? Obviously, Luna was not ready to pop. He ignored Maliyan's suggestion. He tried to ignore his watermelon juice special obsession. He tried to ignore everything. But nothing ignored him. He started feeling worse and worse about himself. And when he got mean to himself, he could also get mean to others.

One of his favourite negative things in that state was to talk about his many other friends. With each additional reference to the long list of "important" friends, Maliyan got further and further down the list. If she had let him, he would have got so dismissive that she would have ended up as a worm (no offence to worms). But she didn't let him. It is one thing to understand that someone's destructive behaviour stems from their loathing of themselves. It is another to accept that behaviour towards oneself. And so, Luna and Maliyan lived in the same house but in disconnected worlds.

# CHAPTER 13

# DORIE'S CAFE

*A* *week later:*
It was nearly 7:00 a.m. as Maliyan passed Paperboy on her morning walk and headed further down the main street to *Dorie's Cafe.*

WHEN SHE MOVED TO THE FLAT, IT TOOK MALIYAN quite a while to visit Dorie's Cafe because it looked so ordinary. It was clean and ordered but outdated, personality-less, and empty. Although it had many rows of indoor and outdoor tables ready for customers, less than 10% of those intended customers ever showed up.

One day, when everything else was closed, Maliyan went into Dorie's Cafe. Dorie was plain in appearance and thought, but humble and kind, and had a natural country feel for what was healthy. The food in the shop was made on the premises by Dorie's husband, so it was fresh and essentially homemade. Dorie told Maliyan that she preferred organic fruit for her shop juices, but it was too expensive. Sometimes, she brought in fruit and vegetables from her own large garden.

"Not enough rain for them to grow well this year," said Dorie.

She chatted with her longtime customers about their families, work problems, and health issues. She was a cheerful, nonjudgmental listener and tried to add little, inane jokes here and there to bounce the conversation along. At one point, the cafe, which opened forty years ago, would have had all the tables and chairs fully occupied.

❧

ON HER SECOND VISIT TO DORIE'S CAFE, MALIYAN WAS asked if she would like a coffee card.

"Sure," said Maliyan.

The hundred or so coffee cards were marked with the customers' first names and kept in a small box on the counter. Once in the box, you were not forgotten.

When Maliyan tried to use the restroom, the automatic motion-detector lights wouldn't detect her. Dorie came to the rescue, and the light turned on immediately.

"You must be a nobody," Dorie said with a chuckle.

She covered her mouth and apologised as if that was a rude thing to say. Rude wasn't in Dorie's makeup. Anyway, there was some truth in Dorie's comment. The detectors could not pick up the form of Maliyan's body. Sometimes, the same thing happened with automatic doors in shopping centres. They couldn't "see" Maliyan, and she would have to wait for someone else to approach the door. Further, Maliyan's fingerprint identity was frequently not recognised on her laptop.

When people are in the process of changing their energetic structure, the normal, physical, Earth-world cues can be missing, reconfigured, or jumbled. You can become a "no-body" in one domain and a somebody in another. The physical body can melt, while the etheric one grows.

*BACK TO THIS MORNING:*

6:00 to 7:00 was tradie time at all the cafes—tradies and early walkers. The front window of Dorie's Cafe faced the sunrise. The pink cloud wisps peeked through the forest-green, causing a watermelon glow. Golden orbs of sunlight stretched their fingers into Dorie's space.

"Bit bright this morning," said Dorie with mild complaint.

"Bloody boss," said an overweight, ageing tradie, interrupting the peace.

He shook his head in disgust as he leaned on the counter and waited for his coffee. Dorie nodded in commiseration.

"Been at it again," said the man. "Always jumping from one thing to another. Never there when we need him. This week, you wouldn't believe it. He started a breathing class here in The Flat. Bloody breathing. I think I know how to breathe, thank you very much!"

The man's belly bobbed around as he laughed in condescending annoyance.

"Tsk, tsk," said Dorie quietly.

She probably also had no idea why someone would need to learn breathing.

"Did you do well with the market crowds last week?" asked Maliyan after the tradie left.

"No, these days we don't open on the weekends," said Dorie with a shrug. "Can't get any staff."

*Luna has no problem getting staff for the weekend,* thought Maliyan, but that was the last thing she would tell her. *Dorie has had her day of business success. Now, she makes a living in a minimally stressful way, and isn't that success enough? Isn't being rich being able to live how we truly want? Life can give us what we need in many more ways than just money.*

# CHAPTER 14

# MAIN STREET MEN

Following the 6:00 to 7:00 a.m. tradie time was the 7:00 to 8:00 *Main Street Men* time. That's what Maliyan called them, anyway. Next door to Dorie's Cafe was another cafe that always had a rowdy group of men aged 50 to 70 who commandeered the outside tables and, to an extent, the whole street. They looked and sounded like builders, plumbers, rescue workers, and other manly jobs, the sort of men who would volunteer for the local C.F.A. (Country Fire Authority), who ran towards fires when everyone else ran away from them. They must have been shift workers, retired, or currently unemployed to afford the luxury of sitting with their mates for an hour every morning.

They told each other stories, jokes, and the occasional bit of news from home. Sometimes, they got carried away with themselves, and you could hear, up and down the street, raucous laughter and snippets of "...chased the f***ing bird...slammed the f***ing door...f***ing fell over... etc." No doubt it was good for their mental health. Men that age can do with a good laugh.

If met on their own along the walking tracks, every one of those men would have politely smiled at Maliyan and said, "Good morning." But here, in the aging schoolyard, they seemed somewhat socially clumsy. They would have responded if Maliyan had stopped and spoken to the group. However, they would have responded with the pack mentality of males viewing females as entertainment. No, thanks. So, every morning, she kept walking.

# CHAPTER 15

## ORCHESTRA

After passing the Main Street Men, Maliyan headed for the most forested section of the walking track next to the creek. It was the first week of autumn, and there was a hint of leaves turning colour. The gravel track made a crunching noise as she went deeper into the grove of oak, cypress, and pine trees —crunch, crunch, crunch. The leaves glimmered as they caught the morning light. Some had a silver backing and turned backwards and forwards like majestic tinsel. Next to the track, the creek jumped here and there over the rocks and through the weeds. It took the path of least resistance around and through the obstacles—bubble, bubble, bubble.

One of the oak trees seemed to be calling. Acorns, mostly green, lay on the ground around it. The magnificent tree emanated a mesmerising, powerful quality. It was partly covered with ivy, making it even more picturesque. Maliyan sat beside the tree, faced the creek, and leaned her back on the trunk. It felt solid and immovable, as if nothing could faze it—as solid as a rock, as solid as the Earth.

Sitting cross-legged against the oak, looking at the lively creek, Maliyan listened. At first, she couldn't hear much. Then, she noticed the wind playing with the leaves of the oak. The wind picked up its intensity, and the leaves moved more energetically—swish, swish, swish. The movement of the leaves harmonised with the bouncing creek—bubble, bubble, bubble.

A new instrument entered the symphony. It was Maliyan's heartbeat. Ba-boom, ba-boom, ba-boom. Leaves, creek, heart. Swish, swish, bubble, bubble, ba-boom, ba-boom. Then, Maliyan's breath joined the orchestra. Breathing in, breathing out. YH (inhale), WH (exhale). Gently and calmly. YH-WH. YH-WH. All four aspects of nature—tree, water, heartbeat, breath—swish, bubble, ba-boom, YH-WH.

As Maliyan breathed out carbon dioxide, the tree breathed it in. As the tree breathed out oxygen, Malayan breathed it in. She breathed out, the tree breathed in, and her spirit seemed to travel into the tree along with the carbon dioxide—into the leaves, along the branches, down the trunk, and into the roots. The oak tree roots were connected to all the other tree roots along the creek. There was an entire root city underground, busily going about its business of transferring food and water and communicating with each member. All was one grand and complex orchestra.

ON THE WAY HOME, MALIYAN NOTICED THAT LUNA HAD taken down the watermelon juice special sign.

Later that day, he bounced in happily, an hour and a half later than usual, and said, "I went for a swim after work and lay in the spa for ages. The water did wonders for me."

With that, he picked up the watermelon tourmaline and took it to the sanctuary of his room.

# SPLITTING PRISM

CHAPTER 16

## BE GONE

Two months of autumn had passed in the cool temperate climate of the ranges. The deciduous trees had had their climactic show of red, orange, and yellow. The winds were now scattering the leaves with be-gone dismissiveness to the far corners of the district.

After speaking with Maliyan at the beginning of the year about Luna's presence in her house, Bell went downhill. Her few connections were long, passive-aggressive messages of psychological explanations, threats to withdraw to "protect" herself, condescending advice about ways in which Maliyan could be more helpful to people, information about how to approach neurodivergent people, and the proper way to affirm and love people in general. They were the masked words of attack.

Bell was such a reactive time-bomb that all Maliyan could do was send a heart emoji, which could have meant anything, thus disarming the escalation. A lesser-aware person would have caved through intimidation, lack of psychological/neurodivergent knowledge, or low self-esteem. A more combative person would have instantly fired up in response to Bell's arrogant and antagonistic approach, and an outright battle of insults would have ensued. Maliyan wondered how such an intelligent person could possibly imagine that her approach (particularly to Maliyan, who clearly cared for her) was a good idea.

Most of Bell's relationships were based on the other person caving, hostile battles, psychological back-patting, uneasy truce, or avoidance. For all Bell's talk of love, she had minimal awareness of Maliyan. She put it down to Maliyan being "closed and unsharing", and said as much. However, a self-assured person does not share in the hope of scraps of love. Sharing is earned by the other's care, which is communicated almost entirely nonverbally. Bell's current approach was doing her far more harm than facing the fear and sense of unworthiness underneath it.

CHAPTER 17

## SHUNYATA

*On planet Shakana, in Maliyan's dream:*

"Hello, Maliyan," said the Wise One telepathically.

"Hello," said Maliyan. "Do you have a name I can call you?"

"Call me Shunyata," said the Wise One. "It means *nothingness*, not in the sense of being absent, but in the sense of fluidity. Nothing sticks to me. I am the feminine half of the Wise Ones."

"Hello, Shunyata," said Maliyan, pleased to have a name.

"Do you remember when we told you about different concurrent realities, last year by your time measurement?" asked Shunyata.

"Yes," said Maliyan. "There is not just one reality, but many simultaneous ones. Although I must admit, that's a difficult concept to get one's head around."

"We understand that," said the Wise One, "but the more you play with the idea, the more sense it will make."

"I have already had glimpses of that," said Maliyan.

"In the version of Earth you are currently experiencing," said Shunyata, "there will be a major splitting of realities."

"What do you mean?"

"Many humans who have chosen Earth, at this time, have done so because they wish to assist in the shift," said Shunyata.

Maliyan's mind went blank. As that tended to happen in the presence of the Wise Ones, she wondered if they purposely blanked out the person's mind so that they were more receptive to new and challenging information.

"Earth is in the process of evolving in two distinct directions," continued Shunyata. "To be accurate, it is evolving in many directions, but for the sake of simplicity, there are two main ones. One is in the positive direction of our planet, ultimately leading to a physical connection between Shakana and Earth and many other advanced planets. The other direction is problematic and may lead to the destruction of your Earth."

"The destruction of which Earth?" asked Maliyan.

"The Earth which is inhabited by those experiencing that particular reality. As I said, there are many versions in between, but these two are the opposing goal posts."

"That sounds... important," said Maliyan.

"Currently, most people on Earth can see both worlds," said Shunyata, "but there is a divider field that could be likened to a glass wall between them. Most people can still choose which side they prefer. With time (as you perceive it), the wall will thicken and become less penetrable."

"Then what?"

"The chasm between the two Earths will broaden, and each version will accelerate towards its future."

"Does that mean we won't see the other goal post anymore?"

"Correct."

"Does it also mean that some people will disappear for us?"

"Yes, it does. Even at this stage, I am sure you have experienced people disappearing from your life out of vibrational incompatibility."

Maliyan thought about people who had disappeared out of her life in that way and wondered what version of Earth they were living on.

"Eventually, in the far distance," said Shunyata, "one version of Earth will become as evolved as we are, where everyone lives peacefully, lovingly, and with a constant experience of happiness, connection, and excitement for life."

"I'm definitely buying that ticket," said Maliyan.

"We hope so," said Shunyata.

Maliyan's smile faded as she thought of her current vibrational incompatibility with Bell.

"Do not grieve the splitting prism," said Shunyata. "People have the freedom to choose the vibration of Earth they want. They are loved by life and can go wherever they wish, positively or negatively. People often have to deeply experience the effect of their choices before kicking goals in the other direction. Be reassured that if your vibration is incompatible with someone else's and they do not want your help, then a splitting of some sort is the best solution. They must choose the world they want to live in. They may not realise that the world they see is their choice, but that does not change that it is."

"Who *will* choose my side of the glass?" asked Maliyan.

"Ahh, we don't want to spoil *all* your surprises," said Shunyata.

CHAPTER 18

# NO TRY, NO GOAL

Feeling that she was moving away from Shakana and returning to Earth, Maliyan held onto the edge of Shunyata's flowing gown.

"One last thing," said Maliyan. "Can you come to me during the day, not just in my dreams. That would be great."

"No," said Shunyata. "You are not ready. You might think you are, but you are not. Our vibration is so much higher than yours, so much more intense, that if we approached you during your waking consciousness, you would go into psychic shock."

"What is that?"

"When an evolved being approaches a lesser-evolved one, the lesser one can experience the contact as energetically overwhelming. All the unresolved issues and blockages in the person will instantly surface as if a magnet is pulling them out. The abrupt force of the experience will be unmanageable, and the person will go into fight or flight mode. They will perceive it as dying. They are not dying, although something does die. The person will usually experience the process with terror. You are in your higher energy state when we come to you in your dreams and meditations. We lower our vibration significantly, and then a meeting in the middle is possible."

"I guess that type of fight or flight reaction can happen between humans, too," said Maliyan.

"Yes," said Shunyata, "if you try to help someone who is not ready, they will run away or fight for survival. That is why respecting people's decisions is vital. Otherwise, you can send them into a version of psychic shock."

"But if I don't try..." said Maliyan

"Intuition and wisdom will guide you," said Shunyata. "And we are closer than you imagine."

# THROWING SHADE

# CHAPTER 19

# RIPE AND READY

In *Paperboy:*

"Ooooh," Luna said to Maliyan, casting his eyes in the direction of a good-looking male customer, who was exiting with his takeaway. "He's ripe for the picking."

As was her general response to such comments, Maliyan ignored him.

Unsatisfied with her non-engagement, Luna persisted, "Don't you think?"

"I don't know," said Maliyan. "Is he? I guess."

Most days, Maliyan called into Paperboy. By now, Luna had formed a close and lively friendship circle with staff members. Taking his cue, they were consistently positive towards her. There were a few gay male customers who were suspicious of her intentions and somewhat jealous of her living arrangement with Luna. They could throw a bit of shade.

Over the past week, every time Maliyan went into Paperboy, Luna made a show of pointing out attractive men to her. Yesterday, he said, "Dayum, somebody call the fire department," when a local firey came in. The day before, he said, "I don't chase men, but I'd trip and fall on that one." Another day, "He's hotter than my ex's karma." Each time he made the comments, he said them to Maliyan within earshot of one of the shady gay men.

# CHAPTER 20

## ENBY

That evening, at home:

"Some of my friends have been commenting about you lately," volunteered Luna.

"Gay friends?" asked Maliyan.

"Uh-huh," said Luna.

"What sort of comments?"

"'Not your usual playlist, hmmm?'" said Luna.

Maliyan laughed and said, "What did you say back?"

"Jealousy's not your colour, babe."

"Did that help?"

"Only for a second."

Maliyan thought for a moment and said, "Tell them I'm non-binary."

"Nah, that won't make any difference," said Luna. "I say you're my housemate."

*A few days later, at Paperboy:*

"Enjoy your oat chai," said Phoenix, as they placed it on the table.

"Oooh, I like your new haircut," said Maliyan.

Phoenix now had a bleach-blonde buzz cut. It perfectly suited their casual look of loose shirt, fitted pants, no makeup, and clean, symmetrical face.

"Thanks," said Phoenix.

"I didn't ever think a buzz cut would work on me, but I always wanted one," said Maliyan.

"Are you enby,*too?" asked Phoenix, glancing in Luna's direction.

Maliyan wasn't sure if they were indicating where they got that information or checking to see if Luna needed them.

"Maybe it's monk DNA from a past life," said Maliyan. Not wanting Phoenix to feel abandoned, she added, "Or maybe I prefer to mix things up so that no one takes anything for granted."

---

* Enby means non-binary.

# CHAPTER 21

# TWO-SPIRIT

S atisfied with the idea that people shouldn't take things for granted, Phoenix took the empty cup away, and Maliyan recalled a conversation with Shunyata.

"The current identity diversity on your planet," said Shunyata, "is helping to break apart destructive, limiting beliefs, which will hold Earth back if not dismantled."

"I guess everyone who is 'different' must have agreed to help with that process," said Maliyan.

"Absolutely," said Shunyata. "Although your current diversity may be somewhat bewildering and even frightening to some humans, it is making way for even greater diversity."

"Such as?" asked Maliyan.

"One day, when you have evolved enough and can cope, humans will come to know that there are many other beings of limitless variety out here in the great unexplored frontier."

"I guess it's not really unexplored," said Maliyan. "It's only unexplored by us."

"Yes, and believe me, when humans start to see the bewildering diversity out here, their small human differences will seem like child's play."

⚜

WHEN PAYING, MALIYAN TOLD PHOENIX, "I'VE HEARD that some indigenous people in North America say that someone who has both masculine and feminine qualities is a Two-Spirit."

"Two-Spirits are healers," said Phoenix.

"They're older than the oldest stories," said Maliyan.

"Ancient as the ancestors," said Phoenix.

"Old-school sacred," piped up Luna, who had excellent hearing.

"Forever fierce," grinned Phoenix to Luna.

"Original edition," shot back Luna. "Limited release."

# DOING IS THE DIALECT

# CHAPTER 22

# SOMEONE SHOULD

Maliyan closed her front door, dumped her dance clothes on the floor, cut up some vegetables for an early dinner, and made a cup of tea. She was hungry and tired. As she slid the vegetables into the oven to roast, she heard a large thumping sound and falling objects. It was coming from the top driveway she shared with her neighbour, Carmel, who once came to her as a client.

Looking through the window, she saw a dump truck unloading about 3 m² of firewood. It sprawled across the entrance of both houses. Next to the woodpile was Carmel's "estranged" husband, Robert, who, like Carmel, was in his late 80s. Carmel recently had an operation, and he was staying with her during the recovery. Maliyan had talked to him several times, and he was a delightful, kind, and caring man with a lot of natural wisdom. Even though Carmel's decision to separate after sixty-eight years of marriage would have been tough for him, he accepted it, held nothing against her, and got on with life.

*Lucky I'm already home from my class,* thought Maliyan, *or I wouldn't be getting into my driveway.*

She put on some track pants, took a sip of tea, and again looked out the window. Robert had started carrying the wood into Carmel's garage. Maliyan glanced at her clock—one hour until dusk. She watched Robert's functioning and determined but clearly ageing body, and sighed her hungry tiredness into her by-now warm lounge room air. She looked out the window for a third time at her neighbours' houses, which contained several strong men.

*Are they going to let him struggle with the wood on his own, at his age, at this time of the day? Someone should help him,* she thought.

Sometimes, Shunyata said,

"Action is the native tongue of Earth."

Maliyan assumed she meant that on other planets and dimensions where physicality was either absent or quasi-present, helping could take many nonphysical forms. But on Earth, because we are a physical planet, our helpfulness needs to be grounded in actually *doing something*. Doing is the dialect of our world.

# CHAPTER 23

# CRACKING THE CODE

"I've come to help," said Maliyan, showing Robert her garden-gloved hands.

He smiled and didn't say no. One of their neighbours, a man in his thirties, got into his expensive car and backed out of his driveway. Maliyan waved, but he purposely didn't look in their direction.

"I thought we were only getting $1$ m$^2$," said Robert, surveying the massive wood pile. "Thanks for helping. It's good to have friends. We'll both throw it into the wheelbarrow, I'll wheel it into the garage, and then we'll make a wood stack. Two hands make light work."

Maliyan wasn't sure it would make light work of this pile, but what else could they do but start and then keep going?

Once in the rhythm of moving wood, Robert started chatting. Even after living in Australia for nearly seventy years, he still had an Irish accent. He came as a twenty-year-old man with his thirty-year-old brother and family.

"Back then, when you were twenty, you were a proper

man," said Robert. "There was no mucking around. You had to support yourself and, before long, a young family."

Although Maliyan suggested they not pile too much wood into the wheelbarrow because it would be too heavy, he insisted, "I'll be right."

"I had such poor schooling," explained Robert, "that when I left school at thirteen, I couldn't read or write. For some reason, I couldn't pick it up, and back then, if you didn't catch on, you were put at the back of the class and forgotten about."

Even now, his words had a sting in them.

"When I came to Australia," he said, "I tried to teach myself to read and write, but it was a struggle. I was trying to learn one word at a time. Once my kids were at school, I watched how they were being taught phonics, which is connecting letters with sounds and blending them together to make a word. So instead of memorising whole words, I learned the secret of sounding them out. I cracked the code of language!"

# CHAPTER 24

# VYING VORTEXES

"My brother and I ended up working as jail wardens," said Robert. "We both spent the rest of our working lives in one or other prison."

The quickest route to the coast from The Flat passed a maximum-security prison. Whenever Maliyan drove by it, she felt an uncomfortable twenty-kilometre radius around the prison, which vibrated with negative energy. It was not just the prison's current energy but the accumulated energy from its history. It was a negative vortex of fear, anger, despair, isolation, and meaninglessness.

The countryside around the prison was notably ugly—flat, cactus-ridden, treeless, dry, and depressing. The open environment was no doubt useful in providing clear sight lines for security and surveillance purposes, but it significantly increased the downward pulling effect of the vortex.

The great saving grace was that to the northwest of the prison, and within its line of sight, was a series of granite ridges, the You Yangs, starkly contrasting the otherwise flat terrain. The You Yangs were a sacred spine of stone and created a powerful positive vortex counteracting the negative vortex of the prison.

There are innumerable energy vortices around the world. Some hold tremendous power, such as Uluru (the sandstone monolith rising majestically from the flat desert plain of Central Australia), but most are comparatively small. Nevertheless, small vortices can still greatly impact our health and sense of well-being. Although we may not know where all the vortices are, we can intuitively find them by living where we feel happy and aligned. Vortices are free energy devices that generate enormous energy without fuel or input, so it's wise to use them.

Some locations can negatively impact us. For example, the high-amplitude, low-frequency vortex of Las Vegas is disturbing to peace seekers. However, it is possible that, by contrast, a person may wake up to their inner light by being saturated with the artificial, outward-pulling, illusory light of the mirage-like city.

CHAPTER 25

# BURNT BLESSING

"When we started at the jails," said Robert, "the death penalty was still operating."

The overloaded wheelbarrow swayed from side to side, but he managed to correct it.

"I saw a lot of dead bodies," he said quietly. "Sometimes, I was on duty in the death yard, the exercise yard for condemned men."

"Oh dear," said Maliyan. "Did you talk to them?"

"Back then, you weren't allowed to talk to the prisoners. You'd get in big trouble if you did. But, to me, they were all just men, not bad men, just people. And I never had any problems with them. Sometimes, I'd say something when I was in the death yard, but we weren't there to comfort them. We were there to make sure they didn't commit suicide before the state hanged them."

That thought was enough to silence them both for several minutes.

"Will we take a break?" suggested Maliyan, gazing at the bottomless pile.

"No, love. You go on inside, but I'll keep going because it'll still be here when I come back out."

As Maliyan continued carting wood, Robert continued talking.

"Some of the men should never have been in prison. Some were in the wrong place at the wrong time. Worse people were walking around free than some who ended up in jail."

"Did anything funny ever happen?" asked Maliyan.

Robert shook his head. "No, nothing funny ever happened."

Maliyan felt that some funny things must surely have happened to both prisoners and wardens, but right now, they had escaped Robert's memory.

Carmel slowly struggled out with her walker and apologised for not helping.

"So lazy!" said Maliyan.

Carmel either wasn't in the mood for a joke or didn't appreciate Maliyan's sense of humour and went back inside with Robert's assurance of, "We're fine, darlin'. Go back inside where it's warm."

"For my first ten years in the prisons," said Robert," I tried to be what I thought wardens were supposed to be. One day, when I came home, Carmel said, 'I don't know where the man I married has gone.' After that, I decided to be myself at work. If they didn't like it, they could sack me. Being someone else was making me miserable."

Another neighbour, a man in his forties, walked past with his two small dogs. He waved hello and pointed to the dogs and the fast-fading light to indicate he couldn't stop to help.

"For a long time, my older brother was a mail censor," said Robert. "He would approve or reject incoming and outgoing prisoner mail. Letters were rejected if suspicious, dangerous, or against prison rules. Sometimes, he would take letters back to the men and say, 'Look here, son. You can't say that to your wife. Fix it up, and then I'll approve it.' Although the prison didn't care about saving marriages, my brother probably saved many!"

As the colours in the western sky dimmed and the blackness encroached, Robert and Maliyan swept away the last of the wood scraps from the driveway. Maliyan then returned to her cup of tea (which was dead cold) and her forgotten vegetables in the oven. They were as black as the night sky outside. She took the smoking tray out of the oven, rescued a few edible potatoes, made a new cup of tea, put some toast on, sat down, and felt that everything was perfectly fine, regardless of burnt dinners.

# PART II
# TIME IS UP

# FORMULA

## CHAPTER 26

## DO SOMETHING

One early July evening:

Six months had passed since Luna began living with Maliyan and the paperboy had "loaned" him the cafe.

"Have you heard anything from the owner of Paperboy?" asked Maliyan.

"Nothing," said Luna.

"Has he returned from Italy yet?"

"No idea."

"Hmm, what's the plan then?"

Luna shrugged and started making dinner.

After he had eaten, Maliyan tried the conversation again.

"What is it you would like to do?" she asked.

"I would like to do something different, but I have to support myself."

"What sort of something?"

"For one thing, I'd like to own a bit of land so that I could be outside."

"You have to be proactive about what you want," said Maliyan. "Otherwise, nothing will happen."

The winter night air was setting in. She turned the heater up and added, "It's fear."

"I'm afraid of having no money!" said Luna.

"You have greater fears," said Maliyan. "Like being laughed at."

"Don't you ever care what people think about you?"

"No. It's my life, not theirs. Besides, most people are in no position to be the judge of anything."

# CHAPTER 27

# IN SYNC WITH SYNCHRONICITY

"Even if I did decide to follow my dreams," said Luna, "my dreams are not going to fund themselves."

"There's another part to the 'follow our dreams' formula," said Maliyan. "We have to follow them in a way that serves other people. Then, one way or another, our dreams will serve us."

"The only serving I know is hospitality."

"That is a belief, not a truth. You don't know what you are capable of until you try. You could organise the cafe schedule so that you had more time to investigate other things. That way, you could test the water and gradually learn to swim in some new medium."

"If I don't work enough at the cafe, I won't have enough money to test any water. I'll be dead. I'll drown."

Maliyan laughed and said, "That is another belief, that abundance means money. Money is only one way for life to give you what you need. There are many other ways. Imagination is one. Time is another. People giving you something is a third. (Didn't the old paperboy give you his cafe for virtually nothing?) And exchange is another one."

Becoming a little excited by the notion that there could be some validity in the idea, Luna offered, "Relationships are built on exchange—money, sex, children, a home, company, love, whatever turns people on."

"Exactly," said Maliyan. "And probably the most important way that life gives us what we need is synchronicity."

"You're losing me on that one," said Luna.

"When we follow our passions, and use them to serve other people, and don't insist on how everything should turn out, life organises the right timing, the right people, the right place, and the right result."

When Maliyan was going to bed, she said, "One more thing, Luna."

"Yes?"

"I have been thinking that when it is spring, I would like to buy a house again. It won't be much because I want to keep some money invested."

"Oh," said Luna, surprised. "I hadn't thought about *you* moving. I guess I've been thinking about what *I* will do. That's selfish, isn't it?"

"You are trying to sort yourself out," said Malayan tolerantly.

Tolerance, however, does not change the need for each person to fulfil their destiny. Maliyan had her own destiny to meet and had to trust that whatever came to her or went from her would work in a positive way, even if it didn't appear so at the time.

"I'll look for somewhere in The Flat," said Maliyan.

Life moves, and we need to move, too. If we understand the synchronistic nature of existence, we'll move in sync with it. If not...then, we'll learn.

YAN YAN GURT

# CHAPTER 28

## SAFETY RATE

**M**aliyan's Uncle Clarence, on the family farm in Yan Yan Gurt (twenty minutes out of Nanima), had been ill and was now recovering. Getting close to ninety, his recovery was probably only going to be partial. So, Maliyan decided to visit him.

Rather than take the small plane to Thubbo, she had the idea to take a slow drive up the beautiful coastal road to the northern city (thirteen hours drive time). Then, she would cross the mountains to drive out west to Nanima (an additional five-hour drive). From Nanima, she would travel to see her uncle a few times before using the faster inland freeway back south again to The Flat (nine hours drive time).

Normally, her trips were well organised in advance, but she wanted this one to be entirely open to synchronicity. She planned neither how long she would be away, how much she would drive each day, where she would stay each night, nor anything else in between. She let synchronicity do all the planning.

When she felt tired from driving, she stopped—sometimes in country towns, sometimes next to a river, park, or forest. Not all the stops were idyllic, although most were. One stop, brought on by a sudden pang of hunger, was in a town which Maliyan assumed would be lovely because it served as a gateway to the natural beauty of a large lakes area and an alpine region.

When Maliyan parked her car, she headed for the grand old building she had just driven past, thinking it would lead to other pleasant buildings. It was a distinctive bluestone Federation structure, with towers reminiscent of European castles and intricate carvings of Australian flora and fauna around its perimeter. However, as she circled the building, Maliyan felt that she was being circled by a group of drug-addled, dishevelled, glassy-eyed folk who seemed to have nothing better to do. It was a courthouse, and today was hearing day.

She wove her way through the crowd, waited at the nearby traffic light, and listened to a sixty-year-old man who was trying to talk his lawyer into getting him out of some predicament. The lawyer was not much more than a boy. He barely looked old enough to have finished law school, and his bored, vacant face indicated little hope for the man's enthusiastic, if muddled, pleas for assistance.

Searching for food was equally undelightful. Every shop looked dirty, and the food options consisted of highly processed, fatty, and old-looking selections that would be more beneficial not to eat than eat. On that note, Maliyan let synchronicity lead her out of the town. She later discovered it had one of the highest crime rates and lowest safety rates in the state. Hungry but unaffected, she recalled Shunyata's glass wall, which, although invisible, had a spotless safety record.

# CHAPTER 29

# UNCLE CLARENCE

*In Yan Yan Gurt:*

On the surface, Uncle Clarence appeared to be a very different person to Maliyan. He was a bush farmer with a lifetime of demanding physical work behind him. He prided himself on his common sense, which Maliyan viewed as not infrequently a lack of education and tolerance more than sense. He was a fierce and loyal protector of his family, land, and sheep. Maliyan's more educated, broad-minded, deep-thinking and subtle alignment with the energetic world was at odds with Uncle Clarence and most bush folk of his generation.

Uncle Clarence's farmhouse was clean and tidy. The fortnightly visit from the subsidised aged care program made a noticeable impact. However, when Maliyan opened his fridge to get milk for a cup of tea, it looked as though it had not been cleaned since his tea-maker had gone down the hill (his wife had died and been buried in the cemetery at the bottom of the hill). The cleaners didn't do fridges, and he must have thought fridges were either self-cleaning or not worth the effort. The shelves were smeared with long-forgotten spills. Half-used jars with ancient use-by dates sported mouldy exteriors. It would have been rude to clean it, so she closed the door and remembered one of her uncle's sayings.

"I don't look at use-by dates. That's what we've got this for!" He would then point to his nose. "Besides, none of you kids ever died!"

He had a way of talking that made every sentence combative. Instead of saying, "I trust my sense of smell," he would stare at you accusingly, point to his nose and say, "That's what this is for," as if it were as plain as the dumb nose on your face. It was a way of saying, "I'm not stupid. You are!" That's why Maliyan always ignored his rather insulting conversational manner. She knew that it was insecurity. His underlying fears made him quick to attack and slow to apologise. Sometimes, when Maliyan was young and they would drive past the wealthier, larger farms, she would ask him, "Do we know them?" He would reply, "No, mate. Bloody oath. They don't talk to the likes of us." Maliyan never did accept the "us" that he was including her in.

They sat outside on the verandah in a patch of warming winter sun. Mornings and evenings in Yan Yan Gurt were as cold as The Flat, but the afternoons were considerably warmer.

"What have you been doing?" asked Maliyan.

Uncle Clarence shrugged and said, "Don't know anyone in Yan Yan Gurt anymore."

That wasn't exactly true, as he knew many families in the area. However, it was true that the town of a few hundred residents had changed significantly over the years. As he no longer had kids or wife to organise his social calendar, he didn't mix with the new town dwellers, and those he did know were becoming fewer and fewer. Besides that, towns, like people, go through stages.

When Maliyan was growing up, Yan Yan Gurt was a hive of community-minded farmers and families. The number of town residents remained the same over the years, but previously Yan Yan Gurt had a highly active community (in good part due to Uncle Clarence's wife). Everyone was involved in everything. "Everything" involved dances, fundraisers, town projects, the tennis club, the pony club, and many other heavily supported activities. However, the children of the town grew up and left for work and marriage, and Uncle Clarence's generation grew older. The next generation didn't take up the slack, and thus, the cycle of the tiny town went into a trough period.

# CHAPTER 30

# DEAD PEOPLE

"**M**y big outing is to the cemetery," said Uncle Clarence.

Maliyan wasn't sure if he was joking, but he wasn't.

"There's nothing for me to do in town. Mrs Benson told me to come to church," he said with a roll of his eyes.

Town consisted of a railway station, two tiny, competing churches, a post office (which functioned a few times a week), a pub, several empty shops, a newly-launched and highly-anticipated general store with groceries, hamburgers, and milkshakes, and an occasionally open internet cafe with tea, sandwiches, and two basic computers, (which was ahead of its time when originally established by Uncle Clarence's wife).

"I can't even go down to the dam," said Uncle Clarence, "because it costs a damn $20 to get in. I was born down there. I should be allowed to get in for free!"

In the 1960s, the Burrendong Dam was built. As the dam filled, it flooded several historic areas. A section of country near Yan Yan Gurt, where Uncle Clarence was born, was one of them and became a pay-to-enter recreation park for skiers, fishers, boaters, and campers.

"So," said Uncle Clarence, "I go down to the cemetery and talk to all my mates."

Maliyan could imagine him walking between the graves of generations of relatives and mates—good exercise, memories, and connection. What did it matter if the connection was with spirits without bodies rather than spirits with bodies? In one sense, we are all "dead people" because we all live in spirit form, whether we have a physical body or not. Or, if you prefer, we are all alive.

# CHAPTER 31

# MICE AND MEN

A neighbouring farmer, a generation younger than Uncle Clarence, pulled up.

"G'day mate," he said. "Just callin' in to see how ya' goin'."

He nodded to Maliyan and then said of Uncle Clarence, "He shouldn't still be here. He's too old to be on a farm."

The neighbouring farmer had a herd of cattle and was planning to retire soon, as he was in his sixties. He wasn't a born-and-bred, three-generational farmer like Uncle Clarence. He moved from the city several decades ago and took pride in his ideas, which he frequently and uninvitedly shared with others.

He was fond of explaining, "I don't look at the weather forecast. I look around me. A few years back, they kept warning of a drought, but the Kurrajongs were flowering. My goats were all having twins, and the kangaroos had one joey on the ground and one, even younger, in the pouch. [Kangaroos can deliberately pause the development of a baby if conditions aren't favourable.] So I knew it would be alright. When it's going to be dry, the ants collect high moisture content food and take it back to their nests, and they weren't doing that."

His ideas weren't new. Many were based on the old understanding of nature and animals "knowing" things ahead of time. What was different was that he didn't unconsciously feel these things in his bones as Uncle Clarence did; he actively sought to identify what they were and then explain them to other people. While he was surely annoying, he was a well-intended man and offered to help Uncle Clarence fix his broken tractor. Uncle Clarence needed the help, so he listened to his neighbour's monologues with an occasional, "Uh-huh."

"At least, the mice are gone," said the farmer as they all ambled towards the tractor. Turning to Maliyan, he explained, "In the plague, I put out lots of buckets of water. The buggers ran up the ramp, fell in the water, and drowned. You couldn't poison them because it would poison the dogs and the wildlife. Then, I put all the dead mice near the ant piles, and by the next day, they were gone."

"I see," said Maliyan screwing up her face.

Uncle Clarence was of the generation where the harsher realities of farming life (mostly death) were kept from children and, to an extent, even from the women.

"You have to work in a seasonally appropriate way," lectured the farmer. "If it's too hot, some jobs have to wait till autumn."

"I just keep workin'," said Uncle Clarence under his breath. "Fruit won't wait. Sheep won't wait."

# CHAPTER 32

## SORRY AND SAD

After the tractor was fixed and the farmer left, Maliyan said, "I'll have to move into the shade. This sun has a bit of bite."

"Bite? It's bloody beautiful!" said Uncle Clarence. "You've lived in the south too long."

After a pause, he said, "I'll have to put the farm on the market soon. It's too lonely here on my own."

He had already sold nearly all of his tens of thousands of sheep and most of the land. The peach orchard had long ago been pulled out. Maliyan gazed at the packing shed below the house where the orchard once flourished. That shed was where she earned her first bit of money and learned a little about the value of hard work. Although the children were probably a blessing and a curse as packing shed staff, it was all hands on deck during the peak summer season. Uncle Clarence still owned the farmhouse, numerous sheds, the house paddocks, and a few sheep (his prize-winning ewe, a sheep with a disability, and a couple of stray sheep friends). Although he complained about his loneliness, he also said that if he lived in a town, he'd be dead in two weeks.

"You don't want to buy it, do you?" asked Uncle Clarence.

"It's my favourite place in the world," said Maliyan honestly, but shook her head. "Besides, we like it when *you* are here, not when you are not."

"I've made a lot of mistakes," he said quietly.

"No..." Maliyan started saying, but then stopped as she realised what he was doing. He had made many, it was true.

"Too many mistakes," he said with a shake of his head.

He didn't want to name those mistakes, but many of them, Maliyan already knew about. She let him be sad. Now was an excellent time to be sorry.

# CHAPTER 33

## SPARKLY BLUE

On the surface, Uncle Clarence appeared to be a very different person to Maliyan. However, as he aged and his fear of dying and regret of past mistakes took centre stage, the two seemed far more alike than they were different. Their DNA had somehow meshed and fused. Death collapses boundaries in a way that life never can.

Why do siblings differ as to which side of the family they will take after in appearance, psychic leanings, aspirations, connectedness, and belonging? A child may love both sides, but their physical and energetic DNA will align more closely with a particular strand running through their generational history.

Maliyan stared into Uncle Clarence's unusually sparkly blue eyes, encased by a seemingly inappropriate, unsparkly, arthritic, almost ninety-year-old body, and the two of them were profoundly more connected than separated. The courage she saw in her uncle's eyes was also hers. It took her not into untamed bushland, but into untamed interior terrain. The same pair of sparkly blue eyes,

Maliyan's and Uncle Clarence's, stared at each other and said goodbye, although sparkly blue eyes can never really say goodbye.

THE NEXT DAY, MALIYAN BEGAN HER DRIVE BACK TO The Flat. She intended to stop somewhere overnight and didn't leave at the crack of dawn. However, synchronicity took control, and she decided to do the whole drive in one day.

At one point, she changed lanes on the freeway and saw that in the lane she had just exited, a large wooden ladder, which must have fallen off a truck, lay strewn across the road. An accident waiting to happen. Synchronicity made sure it didn't happen to her. Hopefully not anyone else either.

As she hadn't left early enough for a one-day drive, it was a race against the winter dusk. Winter won, and the last few hours were in the dark. However, fortuitously, it was full moon. As Maliyan cut across from the freeway to The Flat, crisscrossing the winding, unlit, narrow country roads, the full moon guided her and kept her company, so that she felt her home was not in the distance but with her the entire time.

# UNKNOTTED

# CHAPTER 34

## SOLARA STARLING

*In The Flat:*

"Guess who's getting married?" Luna said a little smugly, one evening.

"No idea," replied Maliyan.

"Dr Tye!"

"Tye?" repeated Maliyan as she tried to process that information. "To who?"

"A woman from Byron Bay," explained Luna. "Her name is Solara Starling—well, I assume that's her adopted name."

He added with a grin, "Her name is probably Sue Smith."

Maliyan smiled and asked, "How do you know?"

"I saw Tye at the pool, and as he has been away all year, I asked him what's been happening?"

At the end of last year, Tye's mother suddenly died. She lived in a town about an hour north of the beach-blessed, wellness-soaked Byron Bay. Her town was a conservative retirement enclave, at least compared to the crystal shops and cafe culture of Byron Bay. At the time, Tye told

Maliyan that he was going to take some time off to process the last few years ("the last few years" meaning the death of his son, his divorce, and now the death of his mother). He said he would most likely stay a while up north after the funeral. And that was the last Maliyan heard of him.

"And what *has* been happening?" asked Maliyan eagerly.

"A lot," said Luna with a wink. "He said that he was living at his mother's house while the probate was processing, and decided to go to a grief retreat in Byron Bay. Solara was the teacher/healer."

Luna put his hands up to indicate no more questions, and that was all he knew.

CHAPTER 35

# HEALING THE HOLLOW

Maliyan decided it was time for a check-up and saw Dr Tye later that week.

"I bet your patients are very glad to have you back," said Maliyan.

Tye smiled humbly and said, "Luna told you my news?"

"Of course," said Maliyan, giving him a hug. "I couldn't be more thrilled for you."

"Thank you," said Tye. "And I hear that Luna is with you these days?"

"As cohabiters," corrected Maliyan. "Not couplers."

"I see," said Tye, who was sure that he wasn't sure about their relationship at all.

Tye then told Maliyan his story. He went to his mother's funeral feeling nothing because he didn't have the space to feel any more loss.

"Living in her home was like living in a tomb," said Tye. "Death and loss and memories haunted me day and night, but for some reason, I couldn't leave. Something in me knew that if I left, I'd be taking the death with me like a shadow. After a few weeks of utter misery, I saw an ad for a grief retreat in Byron Bay. It was called *Healing the Hollow*. As you know, I am by nature a conservative person, but when you hit rock bottom, there's nothing left to lose. Indeed, the retreat began with the words, 'In the fall, may we find our footing.'"

"Tell me about Solara," said Maliyan.

Tye laughed and said, "At first, I thought she was just weird, and I wondered what I had got myself into. But I didn't want to go back to my tomb, so I stuck out the two-week retreat, which was similarly painful to my tomb, but at least there was some chance of...something."

"Hope," offered Maliyan. "Healing."

"Yes," said Tye. "We are very different, but somehow we help each other. I ground her."

He added with a smile, "She probably thinks I weigh her down."

He turned his gaze to the world beyond the window pane, the passing people on the street. When Maliyan first met Tye last year, before she was aware of his personal problems, he cryptically commented about that same window that it was like living in a fishbowl. It no longer seemed fishy in the slightest.

He continued, "And she shows me that life is not what I thought."

CHAPTER 36

# HAVING OURSELVES

*That evening:*

"I'm glad that Tye has someone now," said Luna. "It was sad that he and Leteisha broke up, seeing as they were both good people and got along well. It seemed like pointless pain."

"Being good and getting along are not the markers for staying together," said Maliyan, "and every pain has a point, but I understand what you are saying."

"What are the markers for staying together then?" asked Luna.

"Why should staying together be the goal?" said Maliyan.

"What is the point of getting married then?" said Luna.

*On Shakana:*

Maliyan recalled that on Shakana, no one got married. Marriage was seen as a social convention for planets like Earth. On Shakana, everyone felt deeply connected to

109

everyone, as well as to nature and the very essence of existence. There was no need or desire to seek out special arrangements. Nevertheless, everyone's life path did involve specific people and situations, and that was respected as invaluable for each person's life path.

"Often, we cannot see the pattern of someone's connection to us until the end of our lives," said Shunyata. "We look back and see our paths intertwining over the years and understand the way our matrices were conjoined."

Another time, Shunyata said, "Love is eternal when it is unconditional, but interpersonal arrangements can change, for many reasons. Sometimes, those changes can be mitigated by learning certain lessons. Sometimes, they cannot be. Nevertheless, how a person responds to the changes is always within their realm of power."

❧

"W HAT **IS** THE POINT OF GETTING MARRIED?" REPLIED Maliyan.

"I guess," said Luna, "it can feel comforting to know that someone will be there through thick and thin, even if you act badly, that they're not going to disappear."

Maliyan laughed and said, "If people act badly, isn't it better that they learn not to? Being left is a primary way people learn to behave better."

"True," said Luna.

"Anyway, given that you, *personally,* have such a high propensity towards independence," said Maliyan, "you, *personally*, would easily feel trapped."

After a pause, Luna said, "I think the best solution is for people to wake up every morning and know they are not trapped and neither is the other person, each person can freely choose to be there or not, it is up to each one to make it work, and if someone wants to leave, both people will be fine because, after all, we only ever have ourselves anyway."

"Instead of tying the knot," said Maliyan, "it would serve us all better to practice being unknotted beings."

# ORDERING THE DISORDER

# CHAPTER 37

## BRAIN AND BODY

Three years ago, when Maliyan was living in Nanima, she had a long-term back problem. Eventually, she had surgery for it, which didn't directly fix the issue, but it seemed to go away anyway. Strangely, since starting her healing practice in The Flat, the problem returned with a vengeance and transformed into a neurological functioning problem on the whole right side of her body. It was strange because one would think that when involved in healing work, one would reap the benefits of it oneself.

The neurological issue was the main reason for Maliyan's visit to Dr Tye. As it involved loss of function and shakiness, Tye naturally wanted to send her for scans for all the neurological conditions that affect people over fifty, like Alzheimer's, Parkinson's, dementia, stroke, MS, autoimmune issues, and various other assorted and fun diseases. Although, of course, people should do whatever is helpful and appropriate to them individually, Maliyan didn't want to go for the tests.

"The thing is," she said, "if you don't mind me being

blunt [these days, Tye was far more used to blunt because of Solara], I'm not doing that. I don't like medical tests. They incite fear, and fear feeds disease. If I thought it was necessary, I would go, but I have self-diagnosed myself with FND [Functional Neurological Disorder is a malfunction between brain and body for no apparent reason]. They'll make me go through all the tests with their inadvertent fear-mongering mentality, then they'll say there is nothing wrong with me. Then, I'll tell them that I think it's FND, which many specialists know little about. Then, they'll send me to a movement therapist to learn movements that I am already aware of. And they'll tell me to go to a psychologist. Tye, I can run rings around any psychologist. I'll end up saying something rude."

Tye laughed and said, "Okay, okay. How about this? Go to the chiropractor. That'll clear the nerve pathways and help you to get better brain/body communication."

"Great idea," said Maliyan.

And she did.

# CHAPTER 38

## EXPERIENCING EXPERIENCES

*In Shakana:*

"Could you make my FND go away?" asked Maliyan.

"I could," said Shunyata, "but what would be the point of that?"

"I would feel better."

"Did you go to Earth to 'feel better'?"

Maliyan didn't answer that, so Shunyata continued, "Please remember that your consciousness is not in your body. Your body is in your consciousness. Your true state is that of an expansive spirit, but you chose to have an Earth adventure. A part of your spirit solidified into the construct of your body. When you die, you expand out again to your full-dimensional energetic self. But, for now, you are experiencing the experiences that you wanted to experience for your own purposes."

"What purposes?"

"Growth," said Shunyata. "Like everyone else, you shrank your being into physical form and then got amnesia about who you really are."

"Why would anyone choose to forget such a thing?" asked Maliyan.

"By diving deeply into forgetfulness, you get to experience the abandon and glory of waking up. It's exhilarating!"

Feeling quite unexhilarated, Maliyan said, "I'm trying to reconstruct my body—in my sleep, in meditations and healing—but it isn't working."

"You assume that something is wrong," said Shunyata.

"Hmmm, I would prefer it to go away."

"Let it be what it is. It is there for a reason. Allow it to be that. That is all I can tell you for now, but you are being given all the help you need."

With that, she disappeared, and Malayan woke from her half-meditative, half-dream state.

# CHAPTER 39

# SIGNAL NOT SEEKER

*On Geboor:*

It was a wild, windy, wintery day—perfect for keeping tourists away from the top of Geboor. Maliyan walked its blistery, blowy tracks and went deeper into the towering trees, which were bending and barking in the wind.

Eventually, a voice spoke to her—not out loud, but inwardly, telepathically. Telepathy is not reading someone else's mind. It's a willingness to be on the same wavelength as another person or being. It's picking up on the thought vibrations of the shared territory. People in love do it all the time, and often finish each other's sentences, know what the other is feeling, and mirror their beloved's mind. There are many ways to be in love. If you are in one of them, you will become available to someone else's vibrational frequency.

"My name is Cernunnos," said a voice which seemed to be speaking through the wind and trees. "I am the winter spirit, an elemental. Or, if you prefer, an archetype of regenerative power. In return, for your presence here today, how may I assist you?"

"Can you help me understand the FND I am experiencing?" said Maliyan.

Feeling that that may seem selfish or small-minded when talking to a grand elemental, she added, "If that's okay, I mean..."

Somehow, that seemed even more pathetic. The wind picked up and roared in all directions as if the elemental was scanning her body.

"The FND is not a malfunction, but a recalibration. It is a dismantling of old energetic architecture to make room for a new operating system. Your body is adjusting to a higher vibrational bandwidth. The old pathways of energy, nervous response, and habitual motion are being rewired, and the disruption is part of the upgrade process. Just as a computer can freeze while installing an important update, your body can temporarily lose normal function as it integrates the energetic shift. It isn't dysfunction, it's transmutation. It is the disintegration of an old definition of self that is no longer congruent with your frequency. You are operating at a higher vibration, but remnants of the old identity linger in the physical habits of the body. Your body is resisting the frequency mismatch. The tension must express itself—either emotionally, situationally, or physically—until full alignment is achieved."

After a fertile pause, Cernunnos continued, "The right side of your body is a representation of past templates. As you ascend into a new template of being, a more enlightened state, your right side is dropping the weight of outdated structures. The dysfunction is a refusal to carry the old codes forward. You cannot continue into the next version of reality with the old patterns embedded in your physical matrix. Your nervous system is your interface—both with physical reality and with subtler frequencies. You are clearing static, creating space in the nervous system, and disabling pathways that are no longer relevant to your soul's next steps. Your system is recalibrating to emit higher frequencies, much like a tuning fork."

Maliyan jumped nervously as the trees creaked and cracked loudly under the weight of the wind.

Cernunnos continued, "I came to this mountain to talk to the spirit of Geboor, and I must go now, but remember, there is nothing wrong with you. You are rewiring and shedding timelines. Don't resist the process. It's a coded message from your future self, saying, 'You're ready for more.'

> You are not a seeker.
> You are a signal.
>
> You are not a space holder.
> You are a carrier of frequency.
>
> You are not inviting the light.
> You are the light."

The wind momentarily stopped shrieking, the trees stood still, and Cernunnos was gone.

# SPIRIT OF SPRING

# CHAPTER 40

# HOUSE AND HEART

*Six weeks later, in early spring:*

Although the mornings were still cold in The Flat and mist lingered in the creek hollows beneath Maliyan's home, the late morning spring sunshine breathed warmth into the bones of the town. As Maliyan walked to the shops, golden wattle pom-poms spilled over the foot-paths. Emerging daffodils and jonquils cheered quickening gardens. Magpies sang from fence posts with boldness, and rainbow-coloured rosellas flitted between the gum branches. The previously empty outside tables of Paperboy were now full and flourishing.

Approaching the cafe, Maliyan watched Luna talk to his customers. A trendy city couple with their adult offspring engaged Luna in a bright conversation.

"This honey is divine," said the woman with excessive gesticulation. "Where did you get it?"

Luna shrugged and said, "I don't know, hun, it's probably the cheapest honey I could get."

"Oh," said the woman awkwardly, not being able to think of anything fast enough to rescue her faux pas.

Maliyan smiled at Luna's lack of concern about the woman's pretensions. He began scribbling the orders of some of the shady gay guys.

"Hi, babes," said Luna. "How are we all today?"

"How's your house hunting going?" asked one of them.

"Slowly," replied Luna. "The ones I like are all acreages. Too expensive."

Seeing Maliyan behind Luna, one of them said, "Your housemate is here."

Luna turned to face Maliyan, smiled, turned back to his friends and said, "She's not my housemate, boo. She's my *heart*-mate."

ॐ

*THAT EVENING:*

"It's a bit lonely house hunting on my own," said Luna. "Don't you ever get lonely?"

"No, darling," said Maliyan. "I never feel lonely."

"Oh," said Luna.

Feeling that she had missed a cue, Maliyan asked, "Why?"

"No reason," said Luna, as he went to his room.

ॐ

*THE NEXT MORNING:*

"People like me don't feel lonely," said Maliyan, "because we see things everywhere that other people don't see. It's too busy to feel alone."

Luna didn't want to talk about all the invisible things he couldn't see that apparently kept Maliyan in constant company.

"However, not having the capacity to feel alone," said Maliyan softly, "doesn't mean that I don't enjoy people."

Luna huffed in a dissatisfied way, but kept listening.

"Luna," said Maliyan, "you mean the world to me."

Now, he smiled. Broadly, authentically, emotionally.

"Have a great day," he said as he grabbed his keys. "See you tonight, heart-mate."

## CHAPTER 41

# THE ROAD REMEMBERS

Luna watched the little spring lambs dotted across the paddock. Some were curled up close to their mothers, while others wobbled around on skinny legs, unsure but determined. They were pure white, unlike their mothers, who had dirtier wool. A few jumped and kicked in short bursts, full of energy that they didn't know what to do with. The mothers kept a quiet eye on them, heads down as they grazed, occasionally calling out with a soft bleat. The lambs didn't stray far—always circling back to press into their mothers' bellies.

"It's so peaceful," Luna said to Iggy in the passenger seat, who was also fascinated by the lambs. "And so...new."

They were driving down Station Road, a dirt track not far from The Flat. It led to a now-defunct railway station. The road wound past about fifteen farmsteads. Luna had been to inspect a house that was originally a farmhand's cottage, now on a subdivided five acres. The farm that it once belonged to still operated as a sheep property. Its shearing shed was not far from the farmhand's house.

Further down the road, a middle-aged couple, both on their mobile phones, waved to Luna's passing car.

"Bad phone reception," Luna said to Iggy. "They probably have to stand outside to make calls. Maybe, they think we belong to one of the farms—someone's son or uncle or friend. Not many people would drive down this road."

Old dirt roads have their own tracks worn into them. You have to get to know them and follow the flow of the road, navigating around potholes and avoiding corrugations. If you insist on driving in a straight line, it doesn't work. You have to allow the worn tracks of the road, made from the coming and goings of the farmers, to lead the way. You have to let the road drive you. The road remembers the way.

We may think that if our path in life is not a smooth, upward trajectory, then something is wrong or, at least, it's time inefficient. But if the winding, sometimes erratic, road—the one full of dips and detours—is the one for us, then it will be the most direct route because the smooth one will end up throwing many blocks at us. We often expect progress to look like a clean, upward line, but life generally charts a zigzag course, full of peaks and valleys. The winding path will carry us faster and deeper than the straight one, when it is ours to take.

# CHAPTER 42

# WATCHER'S HOUR

*A* *week later:*

It was 3:00 a.m.—the psychic hour, the watcher's hour—when the veil between the worlds is thin, the soul whispers in the dark, and the interdimensional gate swings wide open. Strange visions drift through the mind, magnetically reorienting consciousness toward other realms.

"You will not hear from me for a while," said Shunyata.

"Why?" asked Maliyan. "I need you."

"You will still have our help," said Shunyata. "We never leave you. But you need to concentrate on other things for a while."

Maliyan remembered that the Wise Ones often said, *"It is not we who leave you, but you who leave us."*

"Everything we have given you is inside you," continued Shunyata, "and we leave you with this last reminder:

1. You are who you are meant to be, and that is enough.
2. Your life is yours to live as you choose.
3. Freedom is your birthright.
4. You are an eternal, timeless being.
5. You are endlessly loved and supported by creation.
6. Time is an illusion. There is only now.
7. Trust the perfect timing of your life. It knows the way.
8. Your needs will always be met.
9. When you insist, you create resistance.
10. You are a channel for love, happiness, and healing.

Practice these principles in all the big and little ways, and we will see you on the other side.

# HEART OF HOME

# CHAPTER 43

# FENCE LINE

Luna and Maliyan walked the boundary fence of the five-acre property Luna had recently inspected. The spring afternoon breathed expectantly around them. The nearby ranges stretched behind—soft ridges, rounded hills, and the peak of Geboor. A breeze carried the scent of wattle and grass. The property was mostly cleared, with scattered gums offering dappled shade. The neighbour's dam shimmered in the light. It was peaceful, but also pregnant.

"The other morning, you said that I mean the world to you," said Luna.

"Yes?" said Maliyan.

"I know that you love me," continued Luna, "but you don't really need me... or anyone."

His words drifted out across the paddock, stolen by the mischievous breeze.

"You are my *link to life*," said Maliyan.

Although Luna didn't understand what Maliyan meant exactly, she said it so definitely that his question seemed to disappear.

"So what do you think?" asked Luna.

They leaned on the wire fence, looking across the paddock. Several ewes grazed near the dam, their lambs close by.

"Gorgeous," said Maliyan.

"The house," scolded Luna.

"Very fixable. Cute and comfortable. What more could you want?"

Luna nodded.

"We can be honest with each other, right?" he said.

"Of course, love. If we're not honest with each other, then who are we even in a relationship with? Not the real us."

He nodded again, slower this time. "Right."

A magpie called from a nearby gum. Several lambs sprang at invisible things, all legs and enthusiasm, their mothers barely glancing up.

"Would you..." asked Luna falteringly. "Be interested in buying it with me?"

"Because it's too much for you... on your own?" questioned Maliyan.

Luna nodded.

"And... we'd be housemates?" Maliyan asked.

"*Heart*-mates," corrected Luna quickly.

"Heart-mates," Maliyan repeated. "Yes, you are my heart-mate."

"I know you don't worry about money," continued Luna, "But I do. And I don't want either of us to get stuck in something we can't manage."

"Yes?"

"So... I had an idea."

"Uh-huh."

"What about a *five-year plan?*" proposed Luna. "It

wouldn't mean we have to stay five years if something really important happened, but it would give us both a safety net. We'd do our best to make it work—for the sake of the property... and each other. After five years, we could reassess and, if necessary, sell the house and move on—none the worse."

"None the worse..." repeated Maliyan.

# CHAPTER 44

# THE WINTER SPIRIT

*On Geboor:*

Now that the weather had turned for the better, the summit of Geboor was drawing its usual gaggle of day-trippers. Maliyan watched them from a distance—tourists of all kinds, from all places, chatting loudly in their home languages, taking cheesy-smiley selfies and moving on, as if the point was simply to tick off another destination rather than actually *be* in one. No one noticed the stillness of the gums, the blue above, or the way the light bounced across the granite boulders.

Fortunately, it wasn't hard to get away from them. They were intent on following the trodden main path. Maliyan took a small track worn by wallabies and solitary seekers. The sound of tourists dropped away. The gums stood tall and still, their trunks pale and peeling, their new leaves a tender green. The wind had softened since winter, though it still held a crisp edge.

She could see the little town of Black Forest below. Nowadays, almost everyone drove up the mountain. But in days gone by, many locals would have walked. She thought about the farmers' children, with cousins in tow, climbing the lower slopes without a second thought—chasing one another through the bush, playing in the gullies, laughing at their silly jokes, never wondering if they belonged there. Of course, they belonged. They belonged so completely that the idea of not belonging never entered their minds.

A sudden breath of cold air brushed the back of Maliyan's neck. It wasn't just the wind that was surprising. It was something else. A different presence.

*Cernunnos*—the Winter Spirit.

Why was he here now? The cold gathered around her, intentional and focused—a portal of sorts.

"My time is done," said Cernunnos. "But I am here to honour the turning, to hand over the season, to mark the threshold between what has been and what is now."

"Are you sad your time is over?" asked Maliyan, although even as the thought formed, she knew it was a foolish question. Grand spirits like Cernunnos don't trifle with the tremblings of human emotion. He was an archetype of strength and independence.

She felt a shift in the air currents, a flick of movement through the trees, some leaves skittering in a small spiral across her feet.

A flippant laugh from the Winter Spirit.

"I do not return from sentiment," said Cernunnos, "but from ancient rhythm—just long enough to pass on the thread of guardianship."

Maliyan's thoughts returned to Luna's proposal yesterday. They needed to make a decision today so that an offer could be made. That's why Maliyan was on Geboor. To listen.

Not explaining the details of what she was talking

about—details she presumed Cernunnos would sense—Maliyan said,

"If I say yes, what happens if it falls apart?"

Cernunnos said nothing.

"What happens if it doesn't?" asked Maliyan.

The sun reflected off a shiny roof below in Black Forest and sent a white beam towards Geboor.

"I understand Luna's fears," she continued. "I have my own. Different ones. I think."

Cernunnos was still silent.

MALIYAN REMEMBERED THAT ON SHAKANA, NO ONE insisted that relationships declare themselves and fit neatly into names and categories. They would not do the disservice to one another of insisting a relationship must be a certain way, for a certain duration, with specific obligations or societal formats.

Almost all beings there lived their connections without fixed names—partnerships of soul, not form. They saw it as a distortion to bind one another to roles or timelines for the comfort of certainty.

They surrendered to the deeper intelligence of Creation's timing—the sacred rhythm that draws people together when the resonance is right, and allows them to part if and when their shared purpose is fulfilled. Although really, it was understood that there could be no true parting.

They let synchronicity guide how their connections began, how long they remained, and when they were ready to evolve or end. Synchronicity carried the blueprint of every meeting: the teaching, the timing, the transformation.

It saw far beyond what the personal mind could grasp, and because of this, they trusted it completely. Whether joy or grief, growth or stillness, synchronicity understood the invisible work being done between people.

Shunyata would sometimes remind Maliyan that the true nature of a relationship was generally not seen in the midst of it. On Shakana, it was often at the end of one's life—when the wide arc of time curved into a quiet overview—that the shape of each connection became clear. The meanings came into focus. What seemed random was revealed as precise. What felt fleeting was seen as complete. Until then, relationships were lived not as defined paths, but as *open, fluid, unlabelled presence.*

"What if he hurts me?" asked Maliyan. "Worse, what if I hurt him?"

"What if he blooms?" said the Winter Spirit.

With the thought of blooming, Cernunnos transmitted the following final words and receded into the realms from which he came.

I am bound to nothing.
Yet, I belong to all.

When the world turns,
I turn too.

I do not cling,
but nor do I drift.

I meet each season with gusto,
and then I say *fare well*.

I do not ask the ice to stay,
nor mourn the thaw of frost.

What falls, falls.
What blooms, blooms.
I offer myself to each in turn.

I carry many a promise,
but I never break vows—
for I am wholly present to what is.

I honour your silence.
I honour your voice.
I honour your yes.
I honour your no.

# CHAPTER 45

# TOURMALINE THREAD

Maliyan pulled up at home, having just returned from Geboor. Ribbons of mauve and rose flooded the dusk sky. The fading light wrapped the paddock and creek below her house in its final statement of the day.

Luna sat cross-legged on the lounge room floor, unusually still. He didn't look up when Maliyan entered. Something was resting in his lap.

Still silent, Luna passed her a small box.

Maliyan looked surprised. Luna was not one to give presents. He barely tolerated receiving them—responding with an uncomfortable, objecting gratitude, as if the gift would saddle him with an eternal obligation to return the favour someday. He had certainly never given Maliyan a gift before.

Inside the box was a necklace, understated in its simple beauty. A fine silver chain with a polished piece of watermelon tourmaline. Rose-pink at the centre, melting into forest-green at the edges—perfectly balanced.

"I know you don't wear jewellery," said Luna.

It was true. She didn't. But she hadn't realised he'd noticed that. She liked the *idea* of jewellery, but every time she wore it, something felt... constricted. As if the object was blocking the flow of energy out from her body. She always ended up taking it off again after a few hours.

"But I had it made anyway," shrugged Luna.

"I love it," said Maliyan.

"It's the watermelon tourmaline you gave me at the end of summer when I was obsessing over something or other," said Luna.

Maliyan recalled Luna's *watermelon-special* obsession at Paperboy. The original crystal came in a box that said,

*Watermelon tourmaline will help you connect with your feelings. It will soften the emotional space around you and bring closeness to your relationships.*

"It changed form," said Luna, picking up the necklace and holding it to the light, "but it's the same crystal of an idea."

Maliyan smiled approvingly.

"You've given it to me before we've made our final decision on the property," said Maliyan.

"On the rare occasion I give a gift," winked Luna, "it's unconditional."

"Well then," said Maliyan, "let's see what we can make of this property in five years."

"Yes, let's see," said Luna with a calm smile. "*And* let's see what we can make of *ourselves.*"

*The End*

# SUMMARY OF NANIMA SERIES

*A contemplative journey of **spiritual evolution, soulful relationships, and the quiet healing power of nature.***

Spanning four deeply personal and spiritually rich books—**Nanima**, **Geboor**, **Sonder**, and **The Flat**—this series follows Maliyan, an insightful and grounded seeker whose path unfolds across the quiet towns and wild landscapes of rural Australia.

Through shifting relationships, ancestral stirrings, and encounters with both seen and unseen guides, Maliyan's life becomes a mirror for our own inner transformation. Alongside her are Luna—intuitive, witty, and playfully avoidant as he learns to love truly—and Bell-Bell, whose brilliance and volatility reflect the challenges of change and the yearning for wholeness.

The *Nanima Series* offers not just a story, but a spiritual companion. It invites you to walk the path of growth gently, to listen deeply to the land and your own spirit, and to remember that evolution is both quiet and profound.

# ABOUT THE AUTHOR

*On top of Mt Macedon (Geboor), overlooking the rural town of Woodend (Black Forest).*

**Donna Goddard** is a spiritual author whose work blends clarity, devotion, and metaphysical insight. With more than twenty published books across spiritual nonfiction, fiction, poetry, and children's literature, she writes to uplift consciousness and offer healing through words.

Donna's Facebook author page has over 400,000 followers from around the world, and her YouTube channel has received more than three million views. Her books are read by spiritual seekers globally and are known for their honesty, poetic style, and transformative energy.

Her writing is an offering—to help others awaken their own inner spirit, trust its guidance, and create a life of depth, beauty, and quiet joy.

All links at https://linktr.ee/donnagoddard

## RATINGS AND REVIEWS

Donna would be most grateful for any ratings or reviews.

# ALSO BY DONNA GODDARD

**Fiction**

*Waldmeer Series: A Spiritual Fiction Series*
*Nanima Series: Spiritual Fiction*
*Riverland Series (children's fiction 6 to 9 years)*
*The Fox Tales (children's fiction 8 to 12 years)*

**Nonfiction**

*Love and Devotion Series*
*Sweet Spirit Series*
*Dance: A Spiritual Affair*
*Writing: A Spiritual Voice*
*Strange Words: Poems and Prayers*
*Love's Longing*
*Master of Me: Meditations*